KOBE BRYANT

BY RAYMOND H. MILLER

KIDHAVEN PRESS™

San Diego • Detroit • New York • San Francisco • Cleveland
New Haven, Conn. • Waterville, Maine • London • Munich

© 2003 by KidHaven Press. KidHaven Press is an imprint of The Gale Group, Inc., a division of Thomson Learning, Inc.

KidHaven™ and Thomson Learning™ are trademarks used herein under license.

For more information, contact
KidHaven Press
27500 Drake Rd.
Farmington Hills, MI 48331-3535
Or you can visit our Internet site at http://www.gale.com

ALL RIGHTS RESERVED.
No part of this work covered by the copyright hereon may be reproduced or used in any form or by any means—graphic, electronic, or mechanical, including photocopying, recording, taping, Web distribution or information storage retrieval systems—without the written permission of the publisher.

LIBRARY OF CONGRESS CATALOGING-IN-PUBLICATION DATA

Miller, Raymond H., 1967–
  Kobe Bryant / by Raymond H. Miller.
    p. cm. — (Stars of sport)
  Includes bibliographical references (p.   ) and index.
  Contents: The right decision—A father named Jelly Bean—Schoolboy star—Straight to the NBA—A new era.
  ISBN 0-7377-1538-3 (lib : alk. paper)
  1. Bryant, Kobe, 1978–Juvenile literature. 2. Basketball players—United States—Biography—Juvenile literature. [1. Bryant, Kobe, 1978– 2. Basketball players. 3. African Americans—Biography.] I. Title. II. Series.
    GV884 .B794 M55 2003
    796.323'092—dc21

2002151092

Printed in the United States of America

Contents

Introduction
The Right Decision 4
Chapter One
A Father Named Jelly Bean 7
Chapter Two
Schoolboy Star 15
Chapter Three
Straight to the NBA 24
Chapter Four
A New Era 33

Notes 41
Glossary 42
For Further Exploration 43
Index 45
Picture Credits 47
About the Author 48

INTRODUCTION

The Right Decision

Kobe Bryant joined the National Basketball Association (NBA) after his senior year of high school in 1996. He became a member of the Los Angeles Lakers, a remarkable achievement. In the previous three decades only six players in the United States had joined the NBA without first playing college basketball.

Kobe was prepared for the jump from high school to the pros. His father, Joe Bryant, had played in the NBA and in Europe for nearly twenty years. Thus, Kobe grew up learning the game from his dad. While in high school Kobe played in pickup games against professional players, which gave him the confidence to compete at the highest level.

It did not take long for Kobe to make his mark in the NBA. He won the slam-dunk competition his rookie

Introduction ★ The Right Decision

Kobe Bryant attempts a defensive steal during a game against the Golden State Warriors.

Kobe Bryant

year, and by age nineteen he was named to the all-star team in the guard position. Known for his outstanding ballhandling and shooting abilities, Kobe teamed with center Shaquille O'Neal to lead the Lakers to three straight NBA titles—all before the age of twenty-four.

Kobe has already been called the next Michael Jordan, which is the ultimate compliment for a basketball player. If he continues to succeed and win championships, there will be no need to compare him to anyone else. He will be in a class all by himself.

CHAPTER ONE

A Father Named Jelly Bean

Kobe Bryant was born on August 23, 1978, in Philadelphia, Pennsylvania. His parents, Joe and Pam Bryant, named him after their favorite restaurant—a Japanese steak house in the Philadelphia area. Kobe was the youngest of three children. He had two older sisters, Shaya and Sharia.

Basketball was a big part of the Bryant family when Kobe was born. His father, nicknamed "Jelly Bean" for his easygoing nature on and off the basketball court, was a star at La Salle University in the mid-1970s and later played forward in the NBA. Although Joe Bryant never became a star in the league, he played a key role for the

Kobe celebrates with his father, Joe "Jelly Bean" Bryant, after winning his first NBA Championship trophy with the Los Angeles Lakers.

Philadelphia 76ers when they made it to the NBA Finals in 1977. At six feet ten inches tall he could handle the ball like a guard, rare for a big man in those days. Kobe's mother's side of the family also had a love for the game. Pam Bryant's brother, John "Chubby" Cox, had a brief

Chapter One ★ A Father Named Jelly Bean

career in the NBA after playing guard at Villanova University and the University of San Francisco.

Kobe loved basketball from the time he could hold a ball in his hands. His parents bought him a miniature hoop, and he spent a lot of his time indoors shooting baskets and pretending he was an NBA star. At age three he told his mother he was going to be a professional player one day, just like his father.

First Love

Kobe loved watching his father play. When he did not attend the games in person with his mother and sisters he set up his hoop in the living room and watched his father play on television. He then imitated his father's moves on the court: If Joe blocked a shot or dunked the ball, Kobe pretended to do the same thing with his little hoop. When Joe drank from a water bottle during a **time-out**, Kobe squirted water into his mouth from his own bottle. When his father used a towel to dry off on the bench, Kobe also used a towel to wipe imaginary sweat from his own face.

Kobe's father was traded to the San Diego Clippers, then joined the Houston Rockets. He retired from the NBA a year later, in 1983. Kobe was six years old. The Rockets' owner was impressed with Joe's personality and business sense, and he offered the former player a job at one of his companies in Houston. Joe accepted the offer because he had to support his family financially, but he soon began to miss playing basketball. He quit his job and moved back home to Philadelphia where he joined

Kobe Bryant

a nonprofessional city basketball league run by Sonny Hill, a legendary basketball figure in the area. Hill had many connections in basketball and arranged Joe's return to the professional game after seeing him play. But the NBA was not where Joe Bryant was headed.

Kobe Bryant leaps up to block a shot by Damon Stoudamire of the Portland Trail Blazers.

Joe Bryant moved his family near Rome (pictured) after signing a contract to play professional basketball in Italy.

Foreign Territory

Kobe's father signed a contract to play in a professional basketball league in Italy. The players there were not as good as players in the NBA, but the league was competitive and the teams paid their players well. That was important to Joe because he wanted to provide his family with a comfortable lifestyle.

Joe did not go to Italy alone. Pam and the three Bryant children moved with him. They lived in Rieti, a small city about forty miles from Rome. Kobe had a difficult time adjusting to life in Italy. Rieti was tiny compared to Philadelphia, and Kobe and his sisters did not speak Italian. To learn the language they spent each afternoon repeating words they heard in school and playing word games. Spending time together, they formed a lasting bond. Kobe and his sisters became best friends.

Within months Kobe could speak the language and was learning to appreciate life in Italy. He loved visiting Rome and other historic places, and he was thrilled when he got to steer a boat through Venice (an Italian city that has canals for streets).

Kobe still had a difficult time making friends, mainly because he and his classmates had little in common. The people of Italy supported their professional basketball teams, but they played the game very little. Basketball was a distant second to soccer, Italy's national sport. Italian children spent their spare time playing in neighborhood soccer matches or kicking a soccer ball around in small groups. Kobe often felt left out.

Shadow Basketball

Kobe did not take to soccer. Basketball remained his favorite sport. He dribbled a ball nearly everywhere he went and shot hoops whenever he could. Sometimes he played a game of one-on-one against an imaginary defender and called the game "shadow basketball." He pretended time was running out in a big game and that he had to make the game-winning shot. He faked one way then another, trying to get his imaginary defender to leave his feet. Then Kobe spun, dribbled, and shot the ball.

When Kobe needed real competition he followed his father to practice. He played on one of the corner hoops as the team scrimmaged. Afterward, Joe spent time teaching

Chapter One ★ A Father Named Jelly Bean

In the style of his favorite player, Magic Johnson, Kobe focuses forward and dribbles past a Cleveland Cavaliers player.

his son moves he had learned in college and the pros. The tips were helpful and Kobe used them immediately. He was often able to coax one of his father's teammates into a game of one-on-one. The player usually took it easy—until he found himself losing to the younger Bryant.

Dreaming of the Lakers

Kobe appreciated European basketball, which emphasized accurate shooting, solid dribbling skills, and teamwork instead of flashy moves, fancy dunks, and being a star. Kobe later explained how learning the European style of play was beneficial to his game. "I started playing basketball [in Italy], which was great, because I learned all the fundamentals first. I think most kids who grow up here in America learn all the fancy dribbling. In Italy, they teach you true fundamentals and leave out all the nonsense."[1]

When Kobe was not watching his father and the Europeans play, he was paying close attention to his favorite NBA team, the Los Angeles Lakers. Kobe's relatives in the United States mailed him videotapes of the Lakers games so he could study his favorite player, Magic Johnson. He idolized Johnson and replayed the tapes over and over. It was his dream to play for the Lakers one day.

Chapter Two

Schoolboy Star

Joe played for several Italian teams and—unlike his days in the NBA—was considered a star everywhere he went. He was among the league's highest scoring players, and the fans adored him. For the rest of the Bryant family, though, life was not as fun. Each time Kobe's father joined another team the family packed up and moved with him. Even between seasons the moving did not stop. The Bryants flew home to Philadelphia to be with their family during the summers when Joe was not playing. The hustle and bustle of professional basketball was hard on the Bryant family. Kobe reflected on the family's many moves and how his mother made the unstable times easier to bear. "My family moved around a lot, going from Italy, Europe, back to the States, so I

Kobe Bryant (center) battles Phoenix Suns defenders for the ball.

was always adjusting to new places, new people. The one thing that never changed was my mother; she's always been there. I'd get up in the morning . . . have those home-cooked meals. And I'd be ready to go."[2]

Each summer in Philadelphia Kobe played in Sonny Hill's city league, where his father once competed. He was

Chapter Two ★ Schoolboy Star

ten years old when he first joined the league, facing players who were often two or even three times older than he was. He struggled at first, but the experience eventually made him a better player. Because he was smaller than the others, Kobe had to outmaneuver his defenders to keep up. For example, he learned where to position himself to take open shots. Competing against stronger players also made him tougher, and he became fearless on the court.

Meanwhile, in 1991 Kobe's father joined a team in France. The team was in financial trouble, though, and on the brink of collapse. Joe played one season then retired from basketball. He moved the family back to Philadelphia so the Bryant children could prepare for college. Kobe was excited to be back in his hometown. Philadelphia was a basketball town and he could not wait to make his mark.

Bold Prediction

Joe and Pam Bryant had kept the children up-to-date on American popular culture through the years by showing them videotapes of *The Cosby Show* and playing music videos. But living in Europe for eight years had changed Kobe, and his knowledge of American culture was not very helpful. He

Kobe poses for a high school yearbook photo. His size and skill with the ball attracted several college coaches and scouts.

17

spoke with an Italian accent, which his classmates found odd. He was also unfamiliar with American slang, so he had a hard time fitting in and making friends at school. That began to change when the other boys and girls saw how talented he was at basketball.

Rumors about Kobe's athletic ability soon began to spread throughout the city, and many of the high school coaches in the area took notice. They were intrigued by the eighth-grader who supposedly had the skills to compete against older players. Being the son of a former pro basketball player only added to their curiosity.

Coach Greg Downer of Lower Merion High School—which Kobe would later attend—was one of the coaches who heard about Kobe. He invited the eighth-grader to scrimmage against the varsity team. For Downer the rumors turned out to be true. Kobe was easily the best player on the court, making most of his shots and outjumping the older players for **rebounds**. The coach predicted that Kobe would one day be playing in the NBA. It was a bold statement considering Kobe was just thirteen years old.

"Ace" on the Court

Kobe made the Lower Merion Aces team as a freshman in 1992, something most high school *sophomores* were unable to do. He quickly showed he belonged on the varsity team when he displayed his unique skills in practice. He beat his defenders to the hoop with moves he used against invisible opponents on the playgrounds in Italy. He also showed flashes of his father as he averaged eighteen

While at Lower Merion, Kobe made the varsity basketball team each season, broke scoring records, and helped the Aces win a state title.

points a game, the most on the team. But the Aces were young and inexperienced, and they finished with a 4-20 record in the suburban Philadelphia Central League.

After his freshman season Kobe practiced on a playground hoop that was six inches shorter than normal. The hoop was perfect for dunking, which Kobe could

19

not yet do on a regulation hoop. He practiced the acrobatic dunks of Michael Jordan and thrilled onlookers with his new talent. After growing to six feet five inches tall at age fifteen, he took his high-flying ability to the Lower Merion gym as a sophomore and amazed fans with his powerful dunks. He averaged twenty-two points a game while leading the Aces to a 16-6 record.

In the summer of 1994 Kobe worked harder than ever on his game. He often played twelve hours a day, participating in six different leagues throughout the week. He was also invited to attend two high-profile basketball camps, where he attracted the attention of college coaches across the nation.

Kobe's scoring average jumped to more than thirty points as a high school junior, and he powered Lower Merion into the state semifinals—one game away from the state championship. The game was close, but the Aces eventually fell 64-59 in overtime to nearby rival Chester. The defeat was especially hard for Kobe who had turned the ball over late in the game with a chance to win. With tears in his eyes he spoke to his teammates afterward and promised to take them one step further the next year.

Pennsylvania's Best

In the summer before Kobe's senior year he attended the prestigious ABCD All-American Camp—a camp only top high school players in the United States were invited to attend. He dominated the other players and was named most valuable player. Kobe's popularity quickly grew, and he was soon among the top recruits in the nation. College coaches

Chapter Two ★ Schoolboy Star

called or wrote daily hoping to convince him to sign an athletic **scholarship**. He surprised them by announcing he was considering skipping college and going straight to the pros. But he made no immediate decisions about basketball after high school—he was too busy playing.

Bryant defends a shot by Allen Iverson of the Philadelphia 76ers during a 2001 NBA Finals game.

Kobe Bryant

Kobe worked his way into pickup games with players of the Philadelphia 76ers at a local university gym. Again he proved he could play against the top competition. In one game he dunked over a taller man. In another game he embarrassed his defender by scoring ten straight points. The player left the court in anger.

Bryant watches as his high school jersey number, 33, is hoisted up and retired in the Lower Merion gymnasium in 2002.

Chapter Two ★ Schoolboy Star

The experience Kobe gained from facing NBA players gave him confidence on the basketball court his senior year. After a slow start, the team went on an incredible twenty-seven-game winning streak that included Kobe's first fifty-point game.

Lower Merion again made it to the state semifinals and faced their old rival, Chester. Trailing by five points late in the game, the Aces came back and took the lead. Kobe sealed the win with a powerful dunk. The team and fans erupted in joy, but there was still one game left in Kobe's high school career.

State Champs

In the Pennsylvania AAAA state championship game Lower Merion faced a disciplined Erie Cathedral Prep team who slowed down the pace and kept Kobe scoreless in the first quarter. He scored eight points in the second quarter, but the Aces trailed 21-15 at halftime. Lower Merion was still losing in the fourth quarter when Kobe led his team to a big comeback. The Aces took the lead and ultimately won the game after Kobe made several key baskets late in the game. This time the team celebrated without reservation. The players took turns cutting down the net. When Kobe's turn came he hung onto the rim and flashed a wide smile, seemingly not wanting the moment to end. But, when the celebration ended, he returned to reality and thinking about the most important decision of his young life: Would he play basketball in college or make the jump from high school to the NBA?

Chapter Three

Straight to the NBA

After winning the state championship and breaking Wilt Chamberlain's forty-year-old southeastern Pennsylvania high school scoring record, Bryant received numerous national awards. He was named to the McDonald's and *Parade* magazine all-American teams, and *USA Today* newspaper honored him with the High School Player of the Year Award. He again talked about turning pro.

Academically, Bryant was a solid student in high school and scored well on his college entrance exam. He could have easily attended a university, gained experience on the court, then turned pro. But his lifelong dream to play in the NBA was growing stronger every day. He knew going straight to the pros after high school would not be

Chapter Three ★ Straight to the NBA

easy, though. Only a player with extraordinary ability could make the transition without college experience.

For several weeks, Bryant talked to his family and high school coach privately about his future. Then on April 29, 1996, at age seventeen, he announced his decision in the

At a 1996 press conference, eighteen-year-old Kobe Bryant announces his decision to skip college and enter the NBA draft.

Lower Merion gym: "I have decided to skip college and take my talents to the NBA. I know I'll have to work extra hard, and I know this is a big step, but I can do it. It's the opportunity of a lifetime. . . . I don't know if I can reach the stars or the moon. If I fall off the cliff, so be it."[3]

Slow Start

Once Bryant announced his decision, several NBA teams flew him in for a workout. One of those teams—the Los Angeles Lakers—was impressed. While measuring his leaping ability the team's coaches were amazed when he jumped and touched the top of the backboard. The vice president of the team said Bryant was the best prospect he had ever seen. He was convinced the high school senior could be a superstar in the league and wanted to select him in the draft. But the Lakers were the twenty-third team to pick in the first round, and Bryant was projected to be drafted much earlier than that.

The Lakers contacted several of the teams ahead of them about a possible draft-day trade for Bryant. The Charlotte Hornets were interested in Lakers center Vlade Divac. So the Hornets selected Bryant with the thirteenth pick, then traded him to the Lakers for Divac. Bryant was ecstatic. His dream of making it to the NBA had come true, and he was going to be playing for his favorite team.

Local newspaper and television reporters covered the Lakers' top draft choice extensively. Even the national media entered the scene and featured Bryant in interviews. The city of Los Angeles was soon buzzing with excitement about the upcoming season. Although the

Kobe shoots over Vlade Divac (left) of the Sacramento Kings. Divac was a key player in the draft-day trade that sent Bryant to the Los Angeles Lakers.

team had not won an NBA title since 1988, when Magic Johnson was playing, Lakers fans were certain Bryant could take them back to the top.

Later that summer Orlando Magic **free agent** Shaquille O'Neal joined the Lakers. The thought of Bryant and twenty-four-year-old O'Neal playing together for years to come gave fans even more hope for the future. The two players were friendly toward one another at first, but they did not become close friends because they had little in common. O'Neal was attracted to the celebrity lifestyle of Los Angeles, while Bryant preferred spending time with his parents. (Joe and Pam Bryant had bought a home in the Los Angeles area.)

Before Bryant put on his number eight Lakers jersey he played on the team's rookie squad. The exhibitions, which usually drew little interest from Los Angeles fans, were to prepare the Lakers' draft picks for the upcoming season. But in 1996, with Bryant playing, the games turned into a showcase event. Fans packed the seats hoping to see the eighteen-year-old in action. He did not disappoint them, scoring twenty-seven points in the first game.

Unfortunately, Bryant's regular season debut with the Lakers was not as successful. Facing the Minnesota Timberwolves, he entered the game as a shooting guard and had his only shot blocked. His slow start continued through the first half of the season. Bryant was unable to find his rhythm because Lakers coach Del Harris was hesitant to play him much more than ten minutes a game. The coach did not feel he was quite ready for the pro game.

Falling Short

Bryant's luck changed when he was asked to play in the rookie all-star game. The game featured the best first-year players from the Western Conference against those from the Eastern Conference. Bryant played almost the entire game for the West and scored thirty-one points. He also electrified the crowd by winning the popular slam-dunk competition.

All-star center Shaquille O'Neal congratulates Kobe Bryant after a Lakers victory in 2001.

Bryant lets a long jump shot fly. Despite a slow rookie season, Kobe quickly developed into one of the league's top scorers.

Chapter Three ★ Straight to the NBA

In the second half of the season Bryant's playing time increased, as did his scoring average. He played an important role toward the end of the season as his teammates looked for him to score in key situations. When the playoffs started, Kobe was playing his best basketball of the year.

In the first two games against the Portland Trail Blazers, Bryant did not play very much. In Game 3, however, the Lakers were losing by thirty-one points and Coach Harris called on Bryant. The rookie responded with exciting dunks and sharp shooting. His play nearly brought the Lakers back, but the rally fell just short.

The Lakers eventually defeated Portland, then met the Utah Jazz in the Western Conference Semifinals. With Los Angeles facing elimination in Game 5, Bryant experienced some rookie growing pains. O'Neal **fouled** out and Bryant attempted to win the game single-handedly. With the score tied he took the game-winning shot, but missed badly. Then, in overtime, he shot three **air balls** from behind the **three-point line** as the Lakers were eliminated. O'Neal spoke to Bryant afterward and told him not to be disappointed. He instructed the rookie to go home, work hard, and get ready for the next season. Bryant did not wait long. He went to the UCLA gym the next day and practiced the shots he had missed the previous night. He was determined to work on his weaknesses and become a star in the league.

Teenage All-Star

Despite Bryant's dismal shooting performance against Utah his popularity increased. Kids loved his style of play, and they imitated his moves on playground courts. Because of his clean image and friendly nature they also saw him as a role model, something that would have put pressure on many nineteen-year-olds. Not Bryant, though. "I love kids . . . I feel very comfortable around them," he said. "Hey, I'm still a kid myself. I think one reason a lot of the kids like me is that they can relate to me. I think a lot of the kids cheering for me these days are people only four, five, six years younger than me. I guess it's an added responsibility for me to be looked up to, but I'll take it. I'll just continue to be myself."[4]

Second Season

In Bryant's second season he was more than just a role model—he was an up-and-coming star. He gained a measure of revenge against Utah by scoring twenty-three points against them in the 1997–1998 season opener. His passing was noticeably better and he played excellent defense. But most of all he had improved his jump shot, his downfall against Utah in the play-offs. Later that season he scored a career-high thirty-three points, including several three-point shots against Michael Jordan and the Chicago Bulls.

Bryant's popularity and improvement was validated when NBA fans voted him to the all-star game as a starter. As the youngest all-star team member in league history, he scored eighteen points and had six rebounds. It was his proudest moment as a professional.

Chapter Four

A New Era

In 1998 and 1999 the Lakers were among the best teams in the league. But both years they were eliminated from the Western Conference Play-offs. In an attempt to push the team to the next level, Los Angeles fired their coach, Kurt Rambis, in 1999. The team then hired former Chicago Bulls coach Phil Jackson.

It was fitting that Jackson was hired as coach. He molded Michael Jordan into a champion ten years earlier. Many people in Los Angeles considered Bryant to be the league's next Michael Jordan, and they hoped Jackson could turn him into a champion, too.

Bryant visited Jackson before the season and asked the coach to let him have a leadership role on the team. But Jackson preferred to build the team around the massive O'Neal. It was the start of an ongoing struggle between Bryant and O'Neal. Despite their differences Los Angeles ended the regular season with sixty-seven

Los Angeles Lakers coach Phil Jackson gives instructions to Bryant on the sideline.

wins—the best record in the NBA. Bryant had his finest season yet, finishing with a scoring average of more than twenty points for the first time.

The Lakers were hard to beat in the play-offs. Bryant hit a last-second shot to defeat the Phoenix Suns, and the Lakers later advanced to the NBA Finals. Facing the Indiana Pacers, Bryant hurt his ankle and missed Game 3, a Lakers loss. He returned in Game 4 and hit several shots in overtime to win the game. Basketball reporters called Bryant's performance "Jordanesque." Two games later Bryant sank the game-clinching **free throws** late in the fourth quarter to seal the Lakers' first NBA title in

Chapter Four ★ A New Era

twelve years. At twenty years old Bryant was a champion—and his critics were silent.

Lakers' Family Feud

Bryant experienced two big changes in his personal life after winning the 2000 NBA Championship. He moved out of his parents' home and bought his own house in Pacific Palisades. And he met a high school senior named Vanessa Lane on the set of a music video. The two hit it off and later got engaged, then married. There were also changes to come on the court.

Bryant, next to his wife Vanessa, waves to fans during a parade celebrating the Lakers' third consecutive NBA Championship title.

When the 2000–2001 season started Bryant tried to take control of the offense by shooting the ball more than he had the previous season. O'Neal, who had been the team's leader since 1996, did not appreciate Bryant's new style of play. The Lakers center tried to reaffirm his leadership role on the team by calling for the ball whenever possible. As the two were unable to hide their differences, news of the feud reached the Los Angeles media, and soon the story went national.

Bryant continued to shoot often and his scoring was up to nearly thirty points a game. But the distraction was threatening to keep the Lakers from their championship hopes. Jackson convinced both players that they could share the spotlight, and he slowly got them to set their differences aside.

Again the team advanced through the play-offs and into the NBA Finals, where they played the Philadelphia 76ers—Joe Bryant's first team in the NBA. After losing Game 1 to the 76ers, Bryant and O'Neal played great together as the Lakers took the next four games to win their second straight title. The two Lakers stars embraced afterward, indicating they truly were over their differences.

"Three-Peat" After Me

Bryant improved every year he had been in the league. His scoring averages in his first five seasons were 7.6, 15.4, 19.9, 22.5, and 28.5. But he did not care about breaking the thirty-point mark in the 2001–2002 season. His goal was to win another NBA title, completing the "three-peat" (three championships in a row). Coach

Kobe steals the ball from Mike Bibby during the 2002 Western Conference Finals, helping lead a Lakers comeback to beat the Kings in seven games.

Jackson had accomplished this remarkable feat twice in the 1990s with the Jordan-led Chicago Bulls.

The other teams in the league did not make it easy for the Lakers. The Sacramento Kings boasted a young, talented lineup that matched up well against Los Angeles. In fact, the Kings ended the regular season with the best record in the NBA, three games ahead of the Lakers. The two teams eventually faced off in the Western

Kobe Bryant's Statistical Averages

Year	Field Goal (percent)	Rebounds per Game	Assists per Game	Points per Game
1996–1997	41.7	1.9	1.3	7.6
1997–1998	42.8	3.1	2.5	15.4
1998–1999	46.5	5.3	3.8	19.9
1999–2000	46.8	6.3	4.9	22.5
2000–2001	46.4	5.9	5.0	28.5
2001–2002	46.9	5.5	5.5	25.2

Source: www.nba.com

Conference Finals. The series went back and forth until Los Angeles was down three games to two and on the brink of elimination. Unable to sleep the night before Game 6, Bryant called O'Neal in the early morning hours and said he was not ready for the season to end. O'Neal agreed and the two promised not to let it happen. That night O'Neal scored forty-one points and Bryant tallied thirty-one in the Lakers' win. The two players again costarred in Game 7 with Bryant hitting several crucial shots as the Lakers barely made it past the Kings to win the series.

Chapter Four ★ A New Era

In the NBA Finals the Lakers were matched against the New Jersey Nets. After the thrilling seven-game series between the Lakers and the Kings, the championship proved to be a letdown. The Nets had no one to stop the Bryant-O'Neal combination. The Lakers beat the Nets in four games.

Kobe Bryant is one of the NBA's best players, and he looks poised to become one of the league's all-time greatest.

Focused on the Present

After Bryant's impressive play in the NBA Finals three years in a row, he was considered by many to be the greatest basketball player in the world—a title Michael Jordan held most of his career. When the Lakers needed a big basket in a crucial situation Bryant usually stepped up to the challenge and came through for the team, just as Jordan was able to do consistently for the Chicago Bulls.

With O'Neal approaching the latter part of his career and Bryant just starting to reach his prime, there is little doubt Bryant will eventually assume the main leadership role with the Lakers. And if he continues to play at his current pace he should come close to—if not break—many NBA scoring records.

Bryant does not discuss whether he thinks he will stand among basketball's all-time greatest players when his career ends, however. He prefers to focus on the present. Once asked about the future, he shook his head and said, "I'm not going to tell anybody that. It's better to keep things like that to yourself. Certain goals you love to share, like winning a championship. Others are to keep yourself interested. I'll just leave it at this: People would be surprised at some of the goals I have."[5]

Notes

Chapter One: A Father Named Jelly Bean
1. Quoted in Roland Lazenby, *Mad Game: The NBA Education of Kobe Bryant*. New York: Contemporary Books, 2000, p. 36.

Chapter Two: Schoolboy Star
2. Quoted in Wayne Coffey, *The Kobe Bryant Story*. New York: Scholastic, 1999, p. 14.

Chapter Three: Straight to the NBA
3. Quoted in Lazenby, *Mad Game*, p. 73.
4. Quoted in Joe Layden, *Kobe: The Story of the NBA's Rising Young Star Kobe Bryant*. New York: HarperPaperbacks, 1998, p. 114.

Chapter Four: A New Era
5. Quoted in Phil Taylor, "Pro Basketball: Boy II Man," *Sports Illustrated*, April 24, 2000, p. 38.

Glossary

air ball: A missed shot that does not touch the rim.

foul: Occurs when a player hits or impedes another player.

free agent: A professional player who is not under contract and is free to sign with another team.

free throw: A shot from the free-throw line that occurs after a foul.

rebound: Occurs when a player gains possession of the ball after a missed shot.

scholarship: A grant of money given to pay a college student's tuition.

three-point line: An arc that, measured from the middle of the basket, is twenty-three feet nine inches at the top and twenty-two feet along the baselines. A field goal made from beyond this line is worth three points.

time-out: What a coach calls to pause play during a game.

For Further Exploration

Books

Wayne Coffey, *The Kobe Bryant Story*. New York: Scholastic, 1999. Examines Bryant's rise from an eighteen-year-old NBA rookie to an established star. Includes photos and career highlights.

Joe Layden, *Kobe: The Story of the NBA's Rising Young Star Kobe Bryant*. New York: HarperPaperbacks, 1998. Provides a detailed look at Bryant's life and career, complete with color photos dating back to high school.

Glen Macnow, *Sports Great: Kobe Bryant*. Berkeley Heights, NJ: Enslow, 2000. A biography that traces Bryant's path in the sport and documents his rise to fame. Includes statistics through the 1998–1999 season.

Robert E. Schnakenberg, *Kobe Bryant*. New York: Chelsea House, 1999. Follows the personal life and career of the Lakers star who turned pro in 1996.

Internet Sources

ESPN.com, "Kobe Bryant." http://sports.espn.go.com. Provides a detailed resource for Bryant's current statistics.

NBA.com, "Kobe Bryant Player Info." www.nba.com. Includes career highlights, game-by-game statistics, a career biography, and more.

Website

The Official Site of the Los Angeles Lakers (www.nba.com). A great source for Lakers news, player info, a game schedule, and more.

Index

ABCD All-American Camp, 20
all-star teams, 6, 32
awards. *See* honors/awards

Bryant, Joe (father)
  basketball lessons from, 12, 14
  career of, 4, 7–8, 9–11, 15, 17
  imitation by Kobe of, 9
  nickname of, 7
Bryant, Kobe
  birth of, 7
  characteristics of, 17, 20
  family of, 7, 11–12
  friends and, 12, 17–18
  in Italy, 11–12, 14, 15
  marriage of, 35
  popularity of, 31–32
Bryant, Pam (mother), 4, 15, 16

Charlotte Hornets, 26
Chester High School, 20, 23
Chicago Bulls, 37
city basketball league, 10, 16–17
college, 20–21, 24–26
Cox, John "Chubby" (uncle), 8–9

Divac, Vlade, 26
Downer, Greg, 18

Erie Cathedral Prep, 23
European basketball, 11, 12, 14

France, 17

Harris, Del, 28, 31
high school, 18–20, 23
Hill, Sonny, 10, 16–17
honors/awards
  all-star teams, 6, 32
  McDonald's all-American team, 24
  Parade all-American team, 24
  rookie all-star team, 28
  slam-dunk competition, 4
  USA Today High School Player of the Year, 24
Houston Rockets, 9

Italy, 11–12

Jackson, Phil, 33, 36–37
Johnson, Magic, 14

Lane, Vanessa, 35

45

Los Angeles Lakers
  desire to play for, 14
  first season with, 28, 31
  NBA championships and, 6, 34–35, 36
  recruited by, 4, 26
  rookie squad of, 28
  second season with, 32
  Western Conference Finals and, 37–39
  Western Conference Semifinals and, 31
Lower Merion Aces, 18–20, 23
Lower Merion High School, 18–20, 23

McDonald's all-American team, 24
Minnesota Timberwolves, 28

National Basketball Association (NBA)
  all-star team, 6, 32
  championships, 6, 34–35, 36
  rookie all-star team, 28
  Western Conference Finals, 37–39
  Western Conference Semifinals, 31
New Jersey Nets, 39

O'Neal, Shaquille
  lifestyle of, 27–28
  NBA championships and, 6
  team leadership and, 33, 36
  Western Conference Finals and, 38
  Western Conference Semifinals and, 31
  one-on-one basketball games, 14

Parade all-American team, 24
Pennsylvania AAAA state championships, 23
Philadelphia
  city basketball league of, 10, 16–17
  living in, 15
Philadelphia 76ers, 8, 22
pickup games, 4, 22

Rambis, Kurt, 33
Rieti, Italy, 11–12
rookie all-star games, 28

Sacramento Kings, 37–38
San Diego Clippers, 9
shadow basketball, 12
slam-dunk competitions, 4
soccer, 12

"three-peat," the, 36–37

USA Today High School Player of the Year, 24

Western Conference Finals, 37–39
Western Conference Semifinals, 31

Picture Credits

Cover photo: Associated Press, AP

© AFP/CORBIS, 27, 34, 35

Associated Press, AP, 5, 10, 13, 21, 22, 25, 29, 37, 39

Classmates.com, 17, 19

© Corel Corporation, 11

© Duomo/CORBIS, 16, 30

Chris Jouan, 38

© Reuters NewMedia Inc./CORBIS, 8

About the Author

Raymond H. Miller is the author of more than fifty nonfiction books for children. He has written on a range of topics, from sports trivia to stamp collecting. He enjoys playing sports and spending time outdoors with his wife and two daughters.